About the Author

Ashante Jones-Gill was born and raised in Lansing, Michigan. He moved to Tennessee continuing his degree in Criminal Justice. Having read many books he began reading J. R. R. Tolkien books in kindergarten that piqued his interest in fantasy, fiction, action and adventure. He is an avid thinker with an imaginative mind. Being a person of morals, principles and values piqued his interest in writing and blending fiction along some of those attributes. Hopefully, this book can be enjoyed by all fantasy lovers, guiding people to make decisions and judgements according to their own sense of what is right and wrong.

Gems of Morality

Ashante Jones-Gill

Gems of Morality

Olympia Publishers
London

www.olympiapublishers.com
OLYMPIA PAPERBACK EDITION

Copyright © Ashante Jones-Gill 2023

The right of Ashante Jones-Gill to be identified as author of
this work has been asserted in accordance with sections 77 and 78 of
the Copyright, Designs and Patents Act 1988.

All Rights Reserved

No reproduction, copy or transmission of this publication
may be made without written permission.
No paragraph of this publication may be reproduced,
copied or transmitted save with the written permission of the publisher,
or in accordance with the provisions
of the Copyright Act 1956 (as amended).

Any person who commits any unauthorized act in relation to
this publication may be liable to criminal
prosecution and civil claims for damage.

A CIP catalogue record for this title is
available from the British Library.

ISBN: 978-1-80439-074-0

This is a work of fiction.
Names, characters, places and incidents originate from the writer's
imagination. Any resemblance to actual persons, living or dead, is
purely coincidental.

First Published in 2023

Olympia Publishers
Tallis House
2 Tallis Street
London
EC4Y 0AB

Printed in Great Britain

Acknowledgements

Thank you to my father Clarence Gill, cousin Dr. Lillie M. Bryant, and my auntie, Min Alfreda Jones-Roby for encouraging me during this process, as well as giving me their advice on the book publishing process, and their own opinions based on books they have published.

Nadir's Life

Living in London, England is one of the wealthiest and most prestigious honors. Known for more than just its remarkable historic buildings and tourist attractions like the London Eye, and numerous art galleries. It is also famous for notable medieval buildings and modern structures that stand in unison and complement each other. Home to some of the largest banks in the UK, such as HSBC and Barclays. However, most of its populous consists of people living in poverty. One of the most affluent citizens living in London is a boy in his twenties named Nadir. Despite this prestigious honor of having wealthy parents, his style of living doesn't show it. Most notably like being driven to and from places in a limo, or having a maid or butler run errands for him. No, the lifestyle he lives is that of any other normal young adult that lives with their parents. He goes to college and comes home, However, before he does anything he goes to the fridge and looks for a small paper sheet. His parents write a list of chores for him to do around the house while they are out of town, or on an errand. He does them without hesitation or procrastination. Swiftly and efficiently, done perfectly. This is a young adult who is the most caring, humble, and righteous person there is despite his wealth. However, no matter how much a person exhibits these traits, no one goes their entire life without being at fault at times, nor are they immune from getting out of character. This is something Nadir will come to learn soon.

London has a famous nickname called "The Big Smoke," referring to the dense fogs and haze that would permeate the city at times. On a random day in the morning throughout the week, the city would live up to that nickname. There was deep fog permeating as well as a massive rainstorm coming down, and it had been carrying on fiercely overnight extending into the morning.

After being done with classes for the day, Nadir is sitting in the back seat of his dad's car after he has picked him up to take him home.

"Another fight again, son."

Nadir, looking at his dad while he was driving, sees that he is distraught and tired.

"I told you never to get into fights! If you are ever feeling the need to get into a confrontation, walk away from the situation! You are better than this, son. This is the third call this week! I don't want you to get kicked out of college. If this keeps happening, we may have to consider homeschooling you. You have a bad temper, son, and you need to learn to control it, otherwise, it will get you into trouble."

Nadir sighs. "I'm sorry, Father, I don't want to keep getting into fights, but if other kids are going to pick on me constantly, I have to stick up for myself and do something!" says Nadir in a rage.

"I get it, son. Trust me, I have been there. You feel like you must stand up for yourself, otherwise, the bullying will continue. However, you must understand, son, people will do things and say things all the time to try and get under your skin, to get a reaction out of you. You cannot allow them to do that. No matter how bad a situation is, you always have a choice to do the right thing and walk away. It is up to you whether you decide to do so."

Nadir looks down, contemplating and processing his father's words.

"Your mother will not be happy about this."

"I know," says Nadir as he looks back up. "I don't want to upset her; I will work on learning to control my temper and I will try walking away next time."

As the drive continues, he looks on and he sees his father shake his head through the rear-view mirror of the car.

"I hope so, son, because this has become a pattern. Your mother and I cannot afford to take you to another college, and that is exactly what will happen if you continue to keep up this behavior. We might have to move to another city as well, and that will cost a lot of money."

"Money isn't an issue for us. We have plenty of it," says Nadir with a chuckle.

"That is not the point, son. Just because we are wealthy does not mean we want to use it every time you make a mistake or get into trouble."

Looking outside the passenger seat window, Nadir sees their home start to appear. Just outside in the front yard, he sees his mother waving at them as they pull into the driveway.

"Ah, it's good to be home," says Nadir as he gets out of the car and stretches his muscles.

His father nods his head in agreement as he steps out of the car. "I could not agree more."

"Hi honey!"

Nadir opens his arms up expecting a big hug, instead, his mother goes past him and straight to his dad and gives him a kiss.

"Gee thanks, Mum." Nadir says as he shakes his head and drops his arms. He then sarcastically says, "Hi honey!"

to his dad.

As his father chuckles, his mum turns to him and says, "Oh stop it, Nadir!" With a smile she says, "Come here!" as she gives him a big hug.

"I'm just joking," he says as they separate from their embrace.

His dad shakes his head with a smile. "So, son, why don't you tell your mum what happened today in class."

Nadir looks at his dad and begins to chuckle. "Thanks for ratting me out." Nadir turns to her mum and sees her mum's demeanor change as she looks at him with an angry disposition and showing her displeasure.

"What happened?"

"Nothing, I just got into a little argument, is all, nothing more, nothing less."

She sighs. "With you there is always something more, so what was the reason behind the argument?

Nadir shakes his head with a sigh. "Fine, I'll tell you. It was about some girl in my class a guy is dating. He's cheating on her. After school, I saw him kissing another girl. I confronted him about it, and he started trying to make excuses for why." Nadir then turns to look at his father. "So I told you part of the story but not all of it entirely. The kids that I told you about, that were picking on me, that was true, but it all stemmed from the argument I had with this guy. Apparently, he is some big-shot popular kid at college. He has some sort of pull on the other kids, so not only do some of the students do what he says, they are also his lackeys or minions in a way. They all pounced on me verbally, and I did so back. There! Are you happy, Mum?" says Nadir as he starts to finally leave the front yard to go inside the house.

"Not quite, she pulls on his shirt before he reaches the

front door. I know you like to help people and stick up for them if you see something that is wrong or being done to them, but you cannot help everyone, sweetie. That girl's situation is not your concern; that is her business. If this guy is cheating and not man enough to tell her, so be it. Even if she is not aware of it, stay out of it…"

"Come on, Mum! Nadir sighs. Maybe you're right, he says as he and his mum walk inside the house. I can't help everybody, and that situation is not my concern. Besides, it's not like me and this girl are even friends. She doesn't even know my name." Nadir chuckles to himself as he walks to his bed and lies down. His mum continues to follow him into his room.

"Hey, I got some homework to catch up on, so I am going to go ahead and get started on it."

"Sure thing, honey, I just wanted to tell you, don't forget there's leftover dinner for you in the fridge."

He laughs. "Please don't remind me!"

"Hey! You will eat it and like it," she says with a smile, as she leaves the room and closes the door behind her.

Nadir then sits up on his bed and opens his laptop while mumbling, "Not likely." As he begins to surf through the web, he stumbles upon an ad for a museum. Interesting, this looks like the kind of place I would like to visit. Let's see here, hours of operations are Monday-Saturday eight a.m.-eight p.m., Sunday twenty-four hours. "Sunday it is," he says, as he shuts the laptop off. He gets ready for bed and goes to sleep.

Gemstone Revealed

The days passed by quickly, and before he knew it, Sunday was here.

"Today's the day," says Nadir as he gets out of his bed and heads downstairs towards the kitchen. "Good morning, Mum, Dad!"

They both turn and look at each other with surprise and say, "Someone is in a good mood this morning."

His dad flips open the newspaper. "Big day today?" he asks while skimming through the paper.

"Well, if you must know, I am going to visit this muse—"

"Well, would you look at this here," his dad cuts him off abruptly. There is a museum that is going to be open for twenty-four hours today! Looks fancy too."

"As I was saying, says Nadir with a sly smile, I am going to visit that museum today."

"What time are you going, and how long are you staying?" they both ask in unison.

"I am going now, it is almost noon, and I will only stay for a few hours. I just want to tour it, that is all."

"OK, well, as long as you are not out too long, it is fine."

"Great! Bye!" says Nadir as he eagerly hurries out the door. "Be back later!" His eagerness to get there was evident because the drive he made when he left his house to the museum took only ten quick minutes when it should have taken at least twenty minutes. As he pulls into a large parking lot and gets out of the car, he gazes at the museum. It is surrounded by a large black gate, and it is the size of a mansion. The color of it is as black as the night sky. It is supported by four large black column pillars, and around the museum is freshly cut grass.

As he makes his way to the door, he sees an elderly man and is greeted, "Welcome to the Gem Museum!" The man was wearing a tailored black suit with black gloves.

"Thank you, sir," says Nadir as he shakes the man's hand. "I saw this museum on TV, and I had to see it for myself."

"Well, sir, you have come to the right place. We have a nice array of gem artwork, and as I am sure you know already by the name of this place, gems!" says the man with a chuckle.

Nadir looks at the man with an intrigued look. "Show me then," he says with a serious and firm demeanor as if he is in control.

"Sure, right this way, sir, we keep several gems in a room here." The man shows him a big white door on a black painted wall. "At the very end of the tour, I will show you them."

"Great, I look forward to seeing them."

"Oh, believe me, sir, once you have seen them, it will forever change your life!"

"Change my life, you say." Nadir chuckles. "Sure, whatever you say."

The rest of the tour seemed to go by quickly, to Nadir it was as if nothing else mattered except the finality of finally getting to see the gems.

"Well, are you ready?"

The man leads him back to the black painted wall again with the white door. On the wall is a painting displaying gemstones. The man simply takes the painting, lifts it slightly, and puts it back in place. Shortly after, a small noise emanates from the wall, and a door slides open leading to a long stairwell.

"No way!" says Nadir, as he stands shocked with excitement and curiosity.

"These gems are so coveted and valuable that we must keep them concealed." The man then begins to lead him down a stairwell, the room in which they were walking down was so dark, the only thing Nadir could do to get a feel for where he was going and keep up, was to literally listen to the sound of the man's voice and try to follow his footsteps. "Here we are." The man stops, and the lights flicker on automatically. He points to a stone tablet with gems gleaming from it. The crystallization on these gems was formed so perfectly it was almost breathtaking. Nadir could not take his eyes off them. There was an array of colors, and they all had a sparkle to them.

"These are incredible!" says Nadir as he picks up one and holds it as if it is the most precious and delicate thing he has ever touched.

"Truly remarkable, aren't they?" says the man with a sly grin. "They are incredibly rare, and before we acquired them, they resided in Egypt."

"What! No way," says Nadir, as he continues to pick up the remaining gemstones to examine them.

"Yes, according to archeologists who found these gems,

their history is quite rich, and dare I say quite magical!"

"Are you telling me these gems have powers?"

Nodding his head, he continues, "Centuries ago, deep in the depths of a pyramid during an expedition in Egypt, there was a gemologist. He was an elderly man who was doing some extensive research on gems there. While doing this, he came across some hieroglyphics. These hieroglyphic markings read that these gems can do anything a man's heart desires. There were five of them there. All you need to do to cultivate their power is focus on what you desire most."

"What? That is ridiculous," says Nadir with a chuckle. "I think you're Bonkers old man."

"Oh, really? Well, I'll tell you what, I will let you borrow one for yourself. Take one and carry it with you throughout your daily life. Then you will begin to understand and see that what I am telling you is the truth."

Fine, why not, he picks up a red gem and puts it in his pocket while thinking to himself, crazy old man. "Well on the bright side, I can show this off to my parents and others at college," he says with a grin. "Thank you, sir, for giving me a tour of this incredible museum. I have to say seeing and hearing about these gemstones was no doubt the highlight of this tour. I want to bring my parents with me the next time I visit and show them this place, I'd think they'd love it!"

"Absolutely, sir, come back anytime!"

"Great, thanks! Bye!" He heads back upstairs to the front entrance of the museum and outside to his car. What a day, I can't wait to share this with my parents. He then gets into his car and leaves through the black gate with a feeling of excitement and curiosity.

The next day, early in the morning, Nadir was in his room, sitting on his bed. Thinking about what the elderly man had told him, he pulls the red gem out of his pocket, stares it over, and then clutches it tight as if it is the most precious thing to him.

He then hears a knock on his bedroom door. "Nadir, breakfast is ready for you downstairs when you're ready."

"OK, thanks Mum." He gets up and leaves his room to go downstairs. As he comes downstairs and walks into the kitchen to sit down and eat, both his mom and dad look at him as if they were both eager reporters trying to find the next big scoop or story.

"Yes?" he says with a chuckle as he looks at them both, "Why are you guys looking at me like that?"

"Well, how did it go?"

"It was good. The museum lived up to its advertisement."

He pulls the gem out of his pocket, gives it a toss in the air, and then tosses it to his dad.

"Check it out," he says with a smile and a proud face. "A gift from the tour guide."

"Well would you look at this. He marvels at it and then gives it to his wife to look at. Here honey."

Looking amazed, she says, "This is beautiful!"

"Thanks! I like it too. There are four more of these back at the museum. I want you guys to come with me when I visit again so you can see them."

"Of course, that sounds like fun. Count your mother and me in!"

"Great! I cannot wait for you guys to see the rest of these gems! OK, I must go. I'm going to be late."

"Have a good day!" they shout as he leaves out the front door to go to school.

Truth Is in the Gemming

Shortly after pulling up to the school, Nadir spots the girl and guy he was telling his parents about last week. Instantly he thinks about the argument he had with the guy. He gets out of the car and glances over to where they are standing and sees that they both are in some sort of heated argument.

"I don't like the way you're acting lately!" she yells. "You have been a completely different person for a few days now!"

"Well, you do not understand! I have a lot going on right now, my grades are slowly slipping, sports are going terribly for me, and I am tired of you questioning every little thing I do! I told you I was going out for a bit, and you ask me question after question, I do not understand why you continue to do this."

Nadir walks pass them, the guy turns his head and catches him looking.

"What the heck are you looking at!" he says with a begrudged look on his face. "Mind your own business!"

"I am trying to, but it is kind of hard to when you're yelling at your girl here."

The guy comes face to face with Nadir and says, "I can do whatever I want to do."

"Oh, believe me, I know you can, you have proven it by what you have already done."

"What did you say!"

"You heard me," he says confidently, staring back at him.

"What is he talking about?" the girl asks with uncertainty in her voice.

"Nothing! I do not know what this guy is talking about. Look, just leave man, this doesn't concern you."

Nadir stands firm and says, "whatever man."

He puts his hands in his pocket and starts to casually walk away. At the same time with his hands in his pockets he grasps the red gem. Suddenly, out of nowhere, he hears a confession from the guy.

Turning back around he hears him say, "I have not been honest with you, there is something I have been keeping from you in fact... I have been seeing another girl."

Nadir quickly turns back around befuddled.

"What?" says the girl in disbelief.

"I did not want to tell you, to be honest I wanted to keep it a secret."

He goes on and on continuing to breakdown everything list by list and Nadir stares in disbelief. As the guy continues to ramble, he then hears his cellphone go off in his pocket. He takes his hand off the gem and then grabs his cellphone to answer the call. The caller ID shows his dad calling him, he starts to answer the phone, but before he could do so he hears the guy finishing up his confession rant.

Suddenly he looks shockingly confused and says, "As I was saying before I got interrupted, everything is fine, I have been stressed out with grades, and sports."

"Are you crazy?" she shouts. "You just told me that you have been cheating on me and lying to me this whole time!"

"Wait, no I did not, when did I say that?"

"You did just now!"

"What?"

"I am done with this." She turns and walks away.

The guy looking on looks baffled and watches her walk away.

"OK, that was nuts," says Nadir. He opens his phone up and sees a text from his dad saying, *we will meet you at the museum when you get out of school.* Nadir shoots him a quick *OK* text and goes inside the school.

Once school ends, Nadir goes to his locker to get the rest of his things. I cannot wait to they see the rest of these gems; he thinks to himself as he grabs his stuff and closes his locker. As soon as he turns around, he runs into the girl he saw earlier, knocking what she was carrying out of her hands.

"Sorry about that!" he says with an embarrassed look on his face as he helps her get her school supplies and bag off the floor.

"It's OK," she says with a smile, "I wasn't really looking where I was going."

They stare at each other for a few seconds before he breaks the silence. "Uh, we haven't met before, I'm Nadir." He chuckles and extends his hand out to shake hers.

"Right," says the girl with a smile, as she reaches out to shake his hand, "My name's Akiza."

"Nice to meet you."

"Same."

"So, how are you doing?" he says with a concerned look. "You had an intense argument earlier today."

She looks up at him with wide eyes.

"You know what, never mind, it is none of my

business."

"No, it's fine! To be honest it has been tough. I am still trying to process it all, I mean I know guys are going to cheat and lie sometimes to try to get away with stuff, that I accept. Our relationship was never on solid ground from the start. What is weird and what I cannot seem to figure out is how he can flat out confess to everything willingly and then afterwards act like he has no recollection of what he said!"

"Yeah, that was crazy!" he says as he pulls out his phone and looks at the time. Realizing he should have left by now he quickly cuts the conversation short. "You know what, that guy was a jerk, he seems like the kind of guy who has no moral ground to stand on when it comes to doing the right thing. He probably was just faking plausible deniability."

"Yeah, maybe," she says with a look on her face as if she is still trying to process it.

"Listen it was nice talking to you, but I really must go!"

"Oh right! Of course, go, I will see you tomorrow then."

"Right, tomorrow." He turns away and begins to run out of the school while he waves bye to her. Smiling back at him, she waves as he heads out the school doors. Racing to the parking lot and getting into his car, Nadir pulls out his phone and sees that his dad has left him another text. *We are here, waiting on you by the front gate, where are you?* Nadir quickly texts him saying *sorry, got caught up at school I am on my way.* After finally arriving to the museum, Nadir sees his parents standing by the museum with annoyed looks on their face.

"Finally, son!" say his parents as he sprints up to the museum door to give them a hug.

"Sorry I am late, just had some stuff going on at class and everything. Let us go in already."

Opening the entrance door to the museum, Nadir sees the elderly man standing right in his way, almost as if he were expecting them to come at that exact point in time.

"Welcome," he says, "come in, come in. Why don't we skip the pleasantries and get straight to the point. Your son invited you here to show you some of our most coveted, and treasured possessions. Our incredible gemstones."

"Yes sir, that is why we are here," says his father as he looks around the museum amazed.

"Well right this way, sir." He directs them to follow him and within no minute's time they are in front of the white door that he showed Nadir when he came touring. He opens the door by sliding back the painting, the door slides open revealing the long staircase towards the very bottom of the museum. Rounding down the circular staircase, they enter the room where the Egyptian stone tablet still resides, and just as they were before, they sit inside the very fabric of the tablet. Nadir's parents notice and quicken their steps over in that direction.

"Incredible, these are amazing," says his father as he picks up one of them.

"Yes, they are honey." She picks up one too.

"Where did you find these?" they ask the elderly man as he starts walking towards them.

"They were found in Egypt, as I told your son, a gemologist was going on an expedition and found these gems during it. Ancient hieroglyphics show that these five gems have powers, which draw on the need or desire of what a person wishes."

They both turn to look at the elderly man in astonishment. "You cannot be serious."

"Oh, I assure you this is no joke. Why in fact, your son has already experienced this firsthand."

"What? No, I have not," says Nadir in shock, "I have yet to see or experience any so-called powers from these gems."

"Are you sure?" he asks, as if he wanted him to really think about his day.

"Well, I thought something weird happened today with this girl and her boyfriend."

Both his parents turn and look at him. "What happened?"

"Well, when I got to school today, I saw the girl I was telling you about and her boyfriend in the front of the school, they were arguing. The girl was trying to get him to tell her what was going on with him because his behavior was not recognizable. Of course, the real reason behind his change of behavior was the fact that he was cheating on her. Like I tried to tell you guys before. He was lying to her, and sure enough when he gave her an explanation it was another lie. However shortly after he lied again, the guy suddenly changed what he said, and started to tell her the truth about everything."

Nadir's parents turn to look at the elderly man with curiousness in their eyes.

"It was weird, I could not believe how quickly he changed his words. And the craziest part about all of this is that when he told her the truth, afterwards he did not even remember what he had said to her. I did not think much of it at the time, I thought the guy was weird anyways, but I have to say I am glad he told the truth. I really wanted him to, enough is enough with all his lies, I cannot stand liars!"

The elderly man chuckles. "You see, remember what I told you, the gem reacts to a man's needs or whatever they desire. You said it yourself; you wanted him to tell the truth to her, he was lying. The gem acted on what you desired."

Nadir stares blankly back. "But that is impossible. How does the gem's power work?"

"Well, it works for you if you wield it in some way. It doesn't matter whether you are holding it in your hand, clutching it, or even wearing it as a pendant or necklace around your neck. If you have it with you, its power is yours. The rest of these gems that you see before you all ready have their own power that will work for you, you must decide on how you will draw on that power. The red gem that you wield right now represents truth and can be calessentially, the others, blue gem is restoration, orange is life, the brown gem is harmony, and the green gem is called comfort. All these gems have qualities that are essential to our way of living. When citizens or people sometimes turn away from these traits or do the opposite, you can change that. Again, it all hinges on your ability to draw these powers out of these gems. When you first visited this museum, I could tell you were a kindhearted, generous, caring and moralistic individual. One that could wield these gems and the powers they possess."

Nadir stares at the red gem he holds still in his hands, as his mom and dad look at him.

Amazed they both say "I cannot believe it." "Who would have thought that when you decided you wanted to check out this museum that you would have this happen to you, son, this is incredible. Just imagine what you could do with these gems, no what you could create!" His dad cannot hold back his jubilated expression.

"Create?" says Nadir with a look of disbelief.

"Yes son, imagine a world without sin, without violence, the very essence of what makes a person, or what they do, can be changed by you."

"I do not even know if I want this, I never said I wanted this!"

The elderly man walks over to Nadir and places a hand on his shoulder. "Sometimes our paths are predetermined for us without us having to do much. I believe you were meant to come to this museum, to be shown these gems. Only someone as kindhearted and pure of heart like yourself can possess these gems. You control all these gems now, son, what you choose to do with them is up to you, however I think I already know what you will set your heart on, to do with them once you leave here."

Nadir suddenly looks up at the old man after staring at the red gem in his hand for so long. "Well, my mother always tells me that I always try to help others and that it is not my job to. Well, Mum. Nadir turns to look at her and smiles. I think it is, and if I can help any person with the power I have been given by these gems, I owe it not only to myself to try, but to the other people out there that may be struggling or in need of a way out. I can be that path of light at the end of the tunnel for them! On the other hand, though… He contemplates his next thought. It may be hard for me to think that I am helping someone and not taking away their free will to do or say whatever they want. I will literally be changing outcomes or essentially what is in a person's heart."

The old man walks over to him and puts his hand on his shoulder. "This is the risk you must take sometimes if you want to profoundly change things."

"Well!" says Nadir's dad as he gets ready to go, "I think we have had enough history lessons today and gem discussions."

"I agree," says Nadir's mum as she prepares to leave. "This is a lot to process, son. Let us go home, and you can rest and think about everything you learned and discussed today."

"Yeah, OK, I am ready," says Nadir as he gathers his things, and the remaining gems from the tablet.

The old man realizes he forgot to say one more thing. "Wait, before you go there's one more thing I forgot to mention. The other gems, their power is not yet active, for you to draw on it you must make the choice on when to use them. The gems power is tied to you, your mind, and your choices. Just as you decided to use the red gem on a situation that involved untruthfulness, its power corrected it by allowing you to hear the truth, which in turn now, the red gem's sole purpose now is to reveal the truth to you."

"I understand," he says as he looks at the remaining gems. "Let us hope I do not have to use them." Finally headed back through the front entrance, Nadir turns around and looks back at the old man. "Thank you for everything."

"No son, thank you, I believe you can do great things with these gems for the better of society."

Nadir smiles at the old man and walks out with his parents and leaves. As the old man watches, he ponders to himself, sadly son, I think you will have to use the other gems, this world is constantly changing for the bad and not the good.

When Nadir finally gets home, he immediately goes to his room and lies down on his bed, contemplating everything that has transpired for him in the past few days. With the gems weighing heavy on his mind, he thinks in his head, can I do this? Can I really impact the world with these gems? He sits up on his bed and takes out the rest of the gems and spreads them out on his bed. Thinking back on what the old man told him back at the museum, he thinks to himself, all these gems, they are connected to me, and their power comes from what I want most. With the red gem I wanted the truth to come out and so the red gem acted on my desire.

All these other gems will have a purpose down the road, I can feel it, says Nadir as he gets up and gets changed ready to go to sleep. He puts all the gems back in a secure tapestry box. I will know what that purpose is soon.

The next morning comes quickly, and Nadir wakes up feeling energized and anxious, ready to tackle the day.

All right, says Nadir as he gets ready for the day. He takes a shower, gets dressed, and finds his tapestry box. Opening it with eagerness, he skims it, grabbing the red gem. I think it will be best for me today if I only take this one, I already know what this gem does, plus it will be easier than trying to carry all the other gems when they serve me no purpose right now. With no powers from them they will be useless to me. Tossing the truth gem up in the air and catching it mid-landing, he says, All right, let's find out what truth will be revealed today. Funny thing about school is there are a lot of kids with emotions running high, sometimes calm, and sometimes livid. The truth can be revealed through both, and I cannot wait to find out what that truth is.

Coming down the stairs for breakfast, Nadir hears his mom calling to him, "Breakfast is ready!"

Entering the kitchen, he sees a plate full of pancakes, eggs, and sausage.

"Hurry up and eat," she says while pouring him a glass of orange juice. "You need to be well fed before you go in today."

"I appreciate this." He scrounges up what he can from the plate and chews swiftly. "I cannot eat all this," he says with a chuckle, "I will finish it all within a day or two."

"OK, I will save the rest in the fridge for you for later then, I am just so excited for you today, and this will be your first day back at school after learning all you did at the museum. In addition to the gems, you now have in your possession. The possibilities of what you can do are endless!"

His dad walks into the kitchen with a smile. "This is all she could talk about last night. I think she wants to do this with you."

"Yeah, I think so too," says Nadir with a laugh. "Even so, this was appointed to me, in fact I still cannot quite understand why or how, all I know for sure is that I want to bring about change and help people in any way I can. These gems can do that for me," he says as he pulls out the red gem from his pocket. "Today the truth will be revealed for some."

Saying bye to his parents, he takes his car and leaves the house for school. When he pulls up to the school, he looks out his car window and sees a vast number of kids interacting with one another.

"Look at all these potential lies possibly being told by these people, underlying and sneaky. I will get to the truth of it all." Nadir steps out of his car and gets the red gemstone out of his box and calmly grips it the palm of his hand. "Well here goes nothing," he says, as he begins to walk up to the school.

Almost immediately as he gets up to the school door to open it, he sees a kid get grabbed by the collar of his shirt and slammed up against a wall by a stout muscular kid wearing a t-shirt, shorts, and a baseball cap.

"Where is my money?" he shouts as he continues to hold him up.

"I told you I would get you the rest of it at the end of the week," says the boy as he looks down at the floor. "Why are you doing this?"

Nadir watches on not too far away from them. "Yes," says Nadir as he firmly grips the red gemstone in his hand and slowly opens the palm of his hand. Why indeed. "Let us find out, shall we?" He chuckles. He grabs the gemstone and holds it out front, pointing it in the direction of the two kids. Suddenly almost as swiftly as the wind blows outside during the day, he sees energy dispel from the gemstone and blow over the two kids instantly. Shortly after that the boy hoisting the kid by the collar gently pulls him down to the ground and lets him go.

After that he says, "I am doing this because I need the money for a family emergency. My cousin is sick right now and she needs medicine. I do not have the money for it right now," he says with a somber mood and tone.

The kid that he let down looks at him with a shocked face as to where his change of demeanor came from suddenly. "Well, I did not know your situation was that urgent, I will try to see what I can do to get you your money before the end of the week. I am sorry to hear about your cousin. I hope that when she gets the medicine she gets well soon."

"Thank you, I appreciate that, and I am sorry for grabbing you like that."

"Hey, no worries, have a good day man."

They both turn away from each other and walk away.

"Well," says Nadir, "that went well, I think. I must admit I thought that kid in the baseball cap was just another bully looking to push a kid around, turns out he was just worried about his family and trying to look after them."

He thinks to himself as he finally gets up to the school doors to walk in, sometimes we might judge someone too quickly. Before we even know the whole story. He looks back down at the red gemstone in his hand. Well, there could always be some underlying truth that is hidden beneath the anger. I hope that kid's cousin gets well sooner rather than later, and as for the other kid, I am glad the truth got out. Nadir then calmly with a slight smile walks into the school. Inside the school Nadir quickly walks to his early morning class. Along the way he sees the girl he helped with her boyfriend standing by her locker getting ready to open it. She starts to turn the lock on it slowly when she notices him out of the corner of her eye still looking over at her.

"Well, hi there," she says as she stops what she is doing. "What are you doing out in the hallway still? Classes are almost getting ready to start, you will be late! And you do not want to be late."

"Well, says Nadir with a sly grin, You may be right, but that is OK. Besides, I am a good student with exceptionally good marks I think it will be OK."

"Oh! is that so?" she says with a chuckle. "You think that will give you some leeway."

"Well, I do not know for sure, but I guess I will find out the truth in a minute or two." Nadir turns away from her and starts to walk to his class door.

The girl watches him leave with curiosity and says, "Good luck! I hope you do not get into trouble."

"Thanks, says Nadir, I should be OK, see you around!"

After finally entering the classroom, he sees every student sitting and they all turn to look at him. In the front of the room, he sees a teacher in a tailored suit sitting at a desk looking over a few sheets of paper on his desk.

Still looking at his papers the teacher says, "Well you are a little late but not too much late because we have not started anything yet." He chuckles. Getting up from the desk he looks in Nadir's direction and says, "take a seat and we will start soon."

"Sure thing," says Nadir with a smile as he finds a seat closer to the back of the room.

"Now that we have our final student in class it is time we get started with our lesson." The teacher faces the class and asks, "can anyone tell me what we discussed last week?" Across the classroom Nadir can see another kid eagerly raising his hand. "Yes Alistair, go ahead."

"Well, we were discussing principles surrounding the concept of morality, what shapes a person." Finishing his statement with firm confidence, he then turns to look at

Nadir.

Thinking in his head Nadir says, "Please, as the teacher begins to reiterate what was discussed while relaying Alistair's clarification to the rest of the class. You remembered something, big deal. Almost everyone in this class remembers the lesson."

"Ethics, says the teacher, Ethics are what gives us the option, or the choice to do what is right or wrong, as in the contrast of good and bad." Nadir looks back at Alistair after he finishes his stare down and sees that he is chuckling a bit as the teacher continues to talk. The teacher finally noticing his silent hysteria, says, "Alistair, do you mind telling the rest of the class what you find so humorous?"

He looks up quickly, caught off guard. "Oh, no," he says with a stern look on his face, "It's nothing."

Nadir thinks, hmm interesting, as he looks on. "Oh, come on," he says with a chuckle as he slowly reaches down in his pocket to grab the truth gem. Clutching it in his fist, he thinks, tell us. The class is eager to know. This is going to be so much fun, not only do I get to put you on the spot, but I can also continue to test out my gem's power. He motions the truth gem in Alistair's direction and light comes gushing from it slowly and envelops him, unbeknownst to the classroom or teacher. Suddenly his demeanor and disposition changes.

Anger takes over his tone. "You want to know what I think, teach! I think ethics being a reason that people do something is a load of crap! Choice is the only sensible reason that people do anything! You either choose to do good or bad. You honestly think that someone's upbringing on ethics plays a role, sure it may play a little part to their moral compass being good. However, ultimately in the end you can try to be the best person you can, while growing up in a loving home, while also being taught well on principles, character, and can still choose the wrong path. I know this, because…" Suddenly, as if Alistair was under a spell, he shakes his head and looks up and around the classroom bewildered. Shocked, he says, "What just happened?" as everyone in the classroom stares at him with a look of disbelief on their face.

A kid shouts from behind him, "You just snapped when the teacher asked you a question about what you were chuckling at."

"No way! You heard me tell him I had nothing to say about it!"

"Well, you did," says another random classmate of his.

Suddenly the teacher breaks the conversation, looking at Alistair with a worried look on his face. "If something is troubling you, you can always come to me after school, or speak to a professional. But I…"

With Alistair still looking befuddled, Nadir looks at him with disbelief, wow I cannot believe he had all that anger pent up inside him, and for me to hear it all! "This gem's power is incredible," he says as he still slightly clutches it in his hand. He begins to put it back in his pocket. Just as he does so, Alistair sees and starts to walk over to him just as the bell rings for class to end. Looking up at him as every student gets up and walks out of the classroom, with the teacher stepping out of the room as well.

"What do you have in your hand, Nadir?" says Alistair with a look of curiosity.

"Nothing! Look, I got to go, but if you want to know so bad, fine!" Nadir fumbles around in his pocket mischievously for something else to show other than the gem. As he does Alistair raises his eyebrows with determination expecting to find out something vital. Alistair then pulls out a stick of gum. "Can never be too cautious with having bad breath," he says with a chuckle. "I like to keep a stick of gum on me sometimes. Want a piece?"

"No!" he says with a look of frustration on his face.

"OK then, see you later," says Nadir as he quickly scurries out of the classroom. Alistair looks on puzzled. As Nadir finally walks outside the school and gets to his car, he thinks to himself, I cannot believe what I heard from Alistair, I had no idea he felt that way, but the thing that was most profound was the anger in his words. It is like there was something deep inside him that was waiting to get let out, and my gem exposed that. If I had known that, I would not have used it for such a selfish reason just to embarrass him. I have got to be more careful with my use of this thing, as he pulls out the gem and admires the gleam from it. Alistair is starting to get suspicious of something, lucky for me he does not even know what he is suspicious of or what to go on. It must stay that way. He opens his car door and gets in to start the ignition and then drives away, leaving the school car park.

Back inside the school, Alistair walks down the hallway wondering how what transpired in class before happened. "I cannot believe it, there is no way I would say something that personal inside a classroom of students let alone anyone else for that matter. What happened to me back there? What was Nadir up to earlier he seemed secretive? Something is going on and I will find out what, he says with a sudden burst of confidence and passion. It better not be anything funny, Nadir, or I will make you pay."

Truth Revealed

The very next day on a cool early morning, Nadir is sitting in a local coffee shop. Not being a big fan of coffee, he walks up to the register and asks for a cuppa. The clerk looks at him funny and says, "A cuppa in the morning?"

"Why not," he says with a small smile. "I need the sugar."

The clerk smiles back and quickly makes a cuppa and hands it to him. As he walks back to his seat and sits down, he overhears a group of adults talking rather discreetly. He finds a menu on his table and pretends to sift through it as he listens in.

"I do not care what," he says. "We need to hit this place tonight, or we will miss our window of opportunity for sure."

"Maybe we will, but it is better than facing him if we screw this up in any way. He is not forgiving; we all know this."

"Hmm," says Nadir as he continues to pretend reading his menu. I need to hear this; this sounds like something that can lead to big trouble. I only need to talk to one of them to get the information I need. All I simply need to do is wait for one of them to leave and follow him. Sure enough, as soon as one of the guys gets up from the table to leave the coffee shop, he gets up and follows him out. The guy has quick feet because as soon as Nadir gets outside, he has already turned a corner down a narrow alley. Nadir catches up to the guy, and as soon as he gets within earshot of him, he shouts, "Hey you!"

The guy whips around, startled, and says, "Who are you?"

"Well, sir, I guess you can say I'm someone that seeks the truth, and I will get what I seek."

The guy, looking bewildered, says, "What?"

Chuckling, Nadir says, "Let me show you."

He reaches down inside his pocket to feel for the truth gem. Once he touches it, it's almost as if the gem and he became complete and in sync with one another. He grips it tightly and quickly whips it out and holds it out in front of the guy's face, with his finger and thumb. Instantly the gem glows and brightens, overflowing the guy's eyes with a red light illuminating from the gem.

"My eyes!" says the man with a screeching pain in his voice as he tries to cover his eyes from the light. However, it is too late, and the gem's light has already engulfed him. After the light dissipates, the guy stands blankly, not moving an inch, almost as if he were transfixed.

"Now tell me," says Nadir with a sternness in his voice, "What are you planning to do to this place I overheard you speaking about earlier in the coffee shop?"

He speaks back now in a soft monotone, saying in almost complete fixation, "We plan on robbing this jewelry store, it's rich in diamonds and we need to score for someone."

"Who is this guy that you need to do this for?"

"We do not know who he is. We have never met him. All we do is get orders from a middleman of his and carry them out."

"Tell me, do you have a way of contacting him?"

"Yeah," says the guy, still in a trance, as he pulls out his cellphone from his pocket. "Here is his number."

Nadir quickly pulls out his phone and punches the middleman's number in his phone. "This is good enough," he says as he puts his phone away. "I have got all the information I need."

He then turns to leave the alley and walks away. As he does so, the effect of the truth gem wears off rather quickly and looking back he sees that the guy has regained focus and his disposition. Chuckling to himself he turns the corner of the alley and says, "Thank you sir, I'd say the truth has set you free."

The next day as he is walking down a busy street in city center he says, "I need to get me a burner phone; using my phone could be risky. I do not know how connected this guy's boss is or how he operates. Best to be safe until I know for sure what I am dealing with."

Later during the day, Nadir quickly buys another phone and starts to text the boss. *Hey, I had to get a new phone. I was approached by a guy last night, and I wanted to be cautious. What is the name of this jewelry store again that we are going to hit?*

He gets a quick reply back, retorting, *I told you already! How many times do I have to say it, Opal!"*

Sorry, I have trouble remembering sometimes, he replies.

Well, get your mind right! We have a big score tomorrow night.

"You won't be scoring anything," he chuckles, "but you

will have a jail appointment." This must be one of the dumbest criminals ever. He does not even ask me, who is this? Or even, how do you have this number? Either he must have a lot of people on this, or he is extremely careless. Whatever the reason does not concern me, the only thing that matters is stopping this planned heist tomorrow.

Wrapping up the text, he says *I know, I'm ready as always, see you there.*

Now all I must do is tip the police in on it. Shortly after the next day came around, night came by quickly. Nadir was sitting on his bed steadily and patiently holding out his phone, looking at it with eagerness.

"Well, it's time," he says as he starts to dial 999.

The 999 dispatcher answers, "What's your emergency?"

"There's going to be a jewelry heist at Opal tonight. You have to send a unit down there now!"

"Hold on, bloke how do you know this? I cannot just send my men out on some technicality or wrong information."

"Never mind how, that is not important. Listen, the information is good! You must trust me."

There is a brief pause on the phone line for about five seconds before the officer says, "All right kid, I'll let the department know, and we will send a few guys out there. This better not be some prank, kid, or you will be in a world of trouble."

"It is not, sir, thank you." He hangs up the phone. Now I think it will serve me best to lay low at home, even though it would be so much fun to go to Opal and watch those guys get arrested. I do not want to expose myself if I do not have to. Imagine the can of worms that will open.

Over at the police station, the dispatcher walks over to another officer.

"Hey, get director bobby, I need to speak with him."

"Sure thing, give me a second."

The director comes out of his office with an annoyed expression on his face. "What is it! I have essential case files that I am looking over, and I keep getting more and more by the day."

"Sir, we got a call about a potential robbery at Opal tonight."

His expression lessens, and a sly smile takes over his face. "Great tip. Who is it from?"

"A kid, well, some guy."

"You cannot be serious. You will take the word of some kid? It could be a prank."

"I assure you, sir, I made sure he knew that, and I told him it better not be, or he'll face severe consequences."

"Do not bring stuff like this to my attention again. We do not have time for this."

"Please sir, I believe we should investigate this; the guy sounded steadfast about this. Plus, this is Opal, one of the most prestigious stores we have. It would not be out of the realm of possibility to think that this might happen."

The chief director turns his head, looking back at the dispatcher with a stern focus. "Fine! We will check it out, and I will take a few guys. If this does not pan out, you owe this entire department a box of custards." He chuckles. He grabs his jacket and walks up to three officers. "You all come with me. We have a potential lead on a heist happening at Opal. I do not need to tell you what potential danger could go down, so be ready, sharp, and focused."

They all say in unison, "Yes Chief!"

"Time to go," he says.

They leave the department and in no time at all, they arrive at Opal.

"We sit tight in the car until I give the go-ahead," he says. He looks around the outside of the building in front and sees nothing. "So far, this kid's lead is not looking good, we may all be in for some doughnuts."

One of the officers in the car says with a chuckle, "Well, I don't know about you guys, but I haven't had a doughnut in a while. I hope we get custard so then I can take at least one box for myself."

Laughter ensues in the car. "Yeah like we will let that happen. And a custard, really? What are you, ten years old? Everyone knows if you want to step into manhood, you must go with chocolate custard with sprinkles."

"Listen, man, that is your prerogative, but do not impose your doughnuts on me."

"Quiet guys," say the chief, "We have two cars approaching."

Two black sports cars pull up in front of Opal, and three guys get out of each vehicle wearing all black with ski masks covering their faces, and they all have guns in their hands.

"Well, no doughnuts for us," says the chief. "Too bad, I was looking forward to it. Radio for some potential backup, we are a little outnumbered."

Shortly after the backup is radioed, they all exit the police car and quietly go towards the front of the Opal building.

"This is going to be one big score, says one of the guys in the ski mask as he rubs his hands excitedly. Just think about all the diamonds we are going to fence."

"No kidding," says another ski-masked robber, "Within a few days, we should get all the money we can muster, and then, of course, we will have to lay low for a few weeks until the heat subsides. Of course, this is not some corner store we are robbing, this is Opal. Only the prestige places for the boss, speaking of, when will he participate in one of these high-end robberies?"

"When it requires him to, he will show up."

"Yeah, yeah, I am just saying we do all the heavy lifting, and he just sits back and chills."

"He has never steered us wrong; he always knows the best places to hit from and when to do it. We have been paid handsomely for our services. Thanks to him, I will have enough money to get all my kids through college and retire off into the sunset, probably live on a beach house in the Bahamas. The proof is in the pudding. He said tonight would be ideal for us to pull this off. No one knows we are here... All right, guys, enough chatter, it is time to do what we came here to do. Let us move."

The robbers move up to the front doors of Opal, break in the glass windows with their guns, and enter. The alarm goes off instantaneously

"OK, hurry!" says one of the guys.

They begin breaking every glass concealment with diamonds and start stuffing them inside their duffle bags.

"We do not have long before the cops get here."

"Freeze!" says the chief police captain as he and the

other three officers have their guns drawn and pointed at the robbers. "Drop your weapons! And the bags!"

"No way!" says one of the robbers. "How are they here already?"

"I am not going to ask you again. I said, drop your weapons!"

"How about no!" Bang! Just as he says it, a loud bang comes from one of the robber's guns, and a cop is down.

"No!" shouts the captain.

Suddenly gun fire ensues. He hurries to the fallen officer while shooting his gun in the direction of the robbers. The rest of the officers fall in line with him and cover him with gunfire.

"Stay with me! You are going to be OK!"

However, it is too late. There is too much blood lost and not enough time for him to stop the bleeding enough to stabilize him and then call in an ambulance for help. The captain then leaves the officer's body with a look of dismay and frustration as he quickly begins to get back into cover and process the current situation. The robbers are able to hold gunfire with the rest of the officers. Without losing anyone, they rush to their getaway cars and speed away from the scene. However, the bag of diamonds that they stole is all there lying on the ground.

With a heavy sigh, the captain says, "Looks like they could not get away with the diamonds, good for us. Gather it all up and call this in!"

"Sure thing, sir," says one of the officers.

"You all know what to do, process the crime scene, and look for anything useful. I will head back to the office. There is something I must do." After getting back to his office, the captain picks up his phone and dials a number.

While sitting on his bed in complete silence, Nadir looks at the truth gem while holding it in his hand and he thinks to himself, I hope they were able to get those robbers. Suddenly his phone starts ringing. Who could this be calling at this hour? It is late. He picks up his phone and looks at the caller ID as it shows an unknown caller. With hesitancy, he answers the phone.

"Who is this?"

"Hi, sorry about the late call. I am a police director."

"How did you get this number?"

"Well, I work at a police station, kid. There are a lot of ways to obtain information, the least of those being a phone number that called in a tip for us."

"Fair enough, what can I do for you, Director?"

"Well, I want to say thank you, your tip was helpful. We had a successful bust."

Suddenly, a red light starts to appear in Nadir's hands. He opens his palm and sees that the truth gem is glowing and illuminating light. What is going on? He thinks, this is happening just like before when I got the truth out of that guy in the alley, I am not doing this. The gem is acting on its own. The red light continues to brighten quickly, and with no time to cover his eyes, it completely takes over him. He opens his eyes. Suddenly, he is standing in front of Opal. Looking befuddled, he looks around Opal and sees the crime scene being processed by officers and crime scene investigators. Including several policemen who are gathered in a circle standing over something on the ground. He walks over to see what it is and sees the dead body of the fallen police officer who was shot. Suddenly, seconds after he sees it, the light pulls him in again, and he is suddenly back in his room, still sitting on his bed. With his palm open, he looks down, and the truth gem is still there but no longer glowing. He thinks to himself, did the truth gem just show me what really happened? It is almost as if it showed me that everything did not go smoothly as the chief told me. Noticing that he still has his phone out and the police chief was still on the line, he quickly focuses back on their conversation.

The chief continues to speak. "We were able to stop the robbers from getting those diamonds, thanks in large part to you. I do not know how you knew this would happen, and I would be remiss if I didn't at least ask, how did you know about this?"

"With all due respect sir, I think how I knew it is irrelevant."

"True, I had to ask though, I am a cop after all," he says with a chuckle. "Well, that is all I wanted to call for. Thank you again for your help."

"Not a problem, sir. I am simply happy that I was able to help."

"Have a goodnight," says the chief director as he hangs up.

"You too, sir," says Nadir as he hangs up and puts his phone down on the bed. A sly smile comes over his face. He gets up and walks over to his dresser. Opening his tapestry, he puts the truth gem in it and slowly locks it up. "That went well. The crime was stopped, as he ponders to himself, but unfortunately what I could not prevent was the killing of that cop. That will be the give and take of this, I suppose. I do not know if I can stop every crime that happens, or prevent outcomes that will potentially follow them. However, what I do know is that I am going to make every effort possible to try. The gem that I do have currently working will allow me to get to and always see the truth in a person, whether that be their mind, thought, desire, action, and even situations. That is very potent. I will build off that, and along the road, I am sure these other gems in my possession will reveal their ability to me or rather as I think of what use they will be to me. This will not be easy, but I must stay the course." He then walks over to his bed and lies down, thinking of all that happened today and what might happen in the days to come.

One evening on a stormy night in London, Alistair is outside walking alongside the sidewalk in a small neighborhood. Deep in thought, he walks over to a newspaper sitting in a small puddle, realizing it by looking at a reflection of himself in the puddle. He walks back to where the newspaper is, picks it up, and opens it. Skimming through it randomly, he flips the pages to an Art and Culture section. Over in the bottom right-hand corner of it, he sees a headline with an address and telephone number underneath saying, "Gem Museum tour offerings, Inquiries about days and times for tour, call this number."

"Hmm," he says with piqued interest, "I did not know that London had a new museum. Well, I am not doing anything this week. Why not call and set up a tour for myself?" While dialing the number to call he thinks to himself, I haven't been to a museum in so long. this should be fun.

An operator picks up on the other line. "Hi and thank you for calling the Gem Museum. How may I assist?"

"Yeah, yeah enough with the cliché speak," he says in a rather hurried annoyance. "Do you have any tour dates available coming up, and what times are available?"

"Well, says the operator, as it turns out, we still have time for one more tour tonight. Seeing as you are in a hurry, why not come on by tonight? You will probably be our only visitor because we are getting close to closing for the night. We have a tour guide ready for you."

"Excellent, I am on my way there now. I will be there shortly."

"Great," says the operator, "See you soon."

Well according to the address given in this paper, I am not too far away from it from where I am now. Time to start walking.

The operator of the museum hangs up the phone with excitement as if he just won the lotto. "Sir, we have one more visitor for you to give a tour to! He will be here soon."

Sitting in a chair in a relaxed state of mind was the elderly man. "Really? You were able to get one more before we closed?" Looking surprised, he stands up and walks over to the operator. "Well done, go home for the night. I will give the last tour for the night and close."

"Sure thing, sir."

"Take the day off tomorrow as well; you have earned it."

"Of course, sir, have a good night."

The operator leaves, and in almost no time at all, the museum doorbell rings. He opens the museum door to see a young adolescent standing with an annoyed and impatient look on his face.

"Hello there, welcome to the Gem Museum."

"Well," says Alistair, "Let's get this over with, you're short on time, and I am as well."

"Certainly sir, right this way."

As the tour continued, it was starting to be a drag for Alistair, who was no more impressed.

"When is this going to be over?" he says with a sigh.

"We are just about done, sir. There is one more thing left I must show you."

"Yeah, and what is that?" he asks with annoyance. "It cannot be any worse than everything else you have shown me thus far."

"Ah, here we are."

They stop at a familiar black wall; the same one Nadir had seen when he was given a tour. Alistair looks at it and sees a similar painting on it showing gemstones.

His eyes finally widen. "Finally, something of interest, this painting is intriguing." As he walks up to it and slowly touches it, suddenly, a similar noise starts to emulate from the wall, and a door slides open. To the surprise of the elderly man, Alistair was not rattled or in awe of what he witnessed, he was rather direct and focused. Fixing his eyes in a stern manner, he asks the man, "What is behind this door?"

"Something only one other guy has seen."

"Another guy? Well, now I must see what is behind it."

"After you."

Alistair begins to walk down the stairwell. Finally coming to a stop at the end of the stairwell, he enters the room and sees a large stone tablet with five empty slots where gemstones had resided.

"I knew that painting on the wall had more significance; the gemstones reflected what gemstones resided on this stone tablet."

"You are correct," says the man, "and down here is where we kept our most prized gemstones."

"So, where are they?"

"Gone."

"What do you mean gone? This is a museum! I mean, isn't everything supposed to be on display? Why remove it?"

"Well, that is the thing, they were not willingly removed, they were given away."

"What! Gemstones just given away. If they are as rare as you say they are, why would you give them away?"

"Well, the gems are rare, like you said, so rare that they contain power."

"What? I do not believe you."

"I assure you, sir, what I'm telling you is true. They can act on your thoughts by channeling what is in your heart, what you desire. The kid who visited before you was just as astonished by what I said and in disbelief, so I let him borrow one to see for himself. As it turns out, the kid came to the realization that I was right and came back to this museum to explain what happened. As a result of his understanding of the power of these gems, I gave him the rest."

"I don't understand, why?"

"I could tell that this individual was kindhearted, generous, and caring. I believed he could do good with these gems, impact change. I believe he has the inner strength to wield and possess these gems, only someone o a pure heart can."

"What? That is crazy! Anyone can possess something if one has the will, strength, and fortitude to do so, I can wield these gems!"

"No, you can't. Sure, you have a good heart, but I feel there is a lot of anger inside you, so much so that if these gems were in your possession, it could be dire and would not impact change in the right way."

"What anger, there is no anger inside me, and what do you mean by impact change? There is no changing the world we live in, a world that is full of hate and bad choices being made by people. People who claim to have a moral compass and ethics. In the end, choice is the only logical conclusion for why bad things happen in this world, robbery, murder, abortion, etc. it all revolves around choice. You cannot impact change when there's choice involved in everything." With the finality of his words, he turns around and looks at the old man with satisfaction. "I have heard enough, and I think I got what I came for," he says with a chuckle. "I do not believe in your ridiculous notion about impacting change with these gems. Still, I do believe you when you say they contain power." He turns to leave, walking back up the staircase. "Good day, sir."

As he walks out of the museum, he thinks to himself, I do not know who that old man gave these gems to, but I will find him, and when I do, I will take these gems or at least one of them for myself. When I do, I will not use them to impact change, I will use them to expose the true darkness that is in a person's heart because, in the end, no one can hide who they truly are or the bad choices they choose to make, while hiding behind ethics.